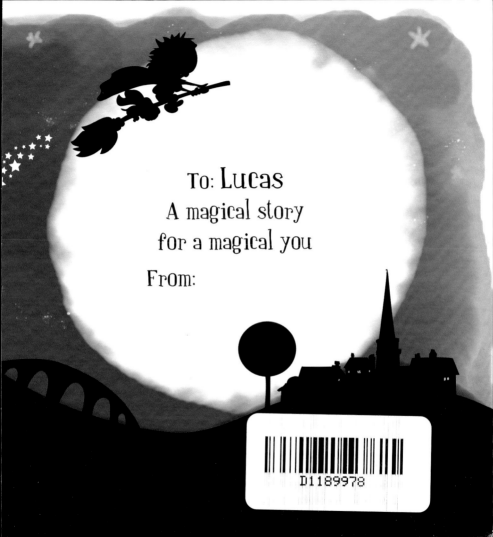

To: Lucas
A magical story
for a magical you

From:

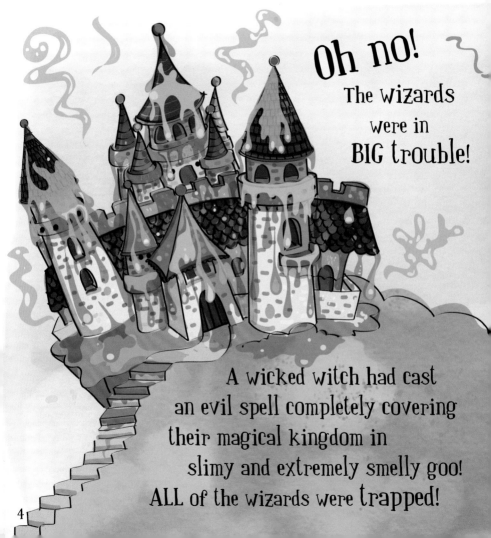

Oh no!
The wizards
were in
BIG trouble!

A wicked witch had cast
an evil spell completely covering
their magical kingdom in
slimy and extremely smelly goo!
ALL of the wizards were trapped!

4

The wizards really needed someone to help them catch the wicked witch, but **who?**

5

The wise old grand wizard looked through his special telescope, and spotted someone who might just be able to help them.

"Quickly! Send Magical Master Owl to ask for Lucas's help in saving us from the wicked witch!" shouted the wizard.

6

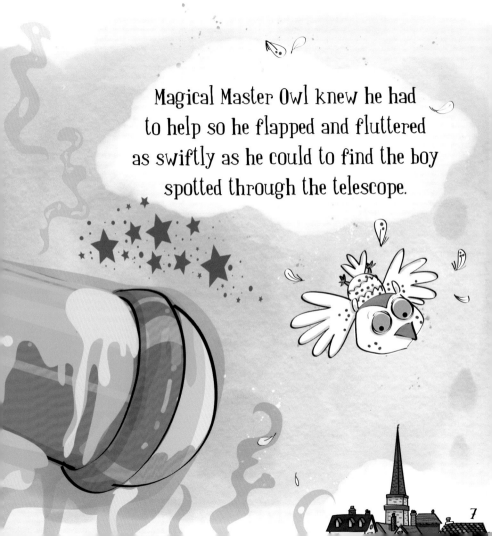

Magical Master Owl knew he had to help so he flapped and fluttered as swiftly as he could to find the boy spotted through the telescope.

7

"WHIZZ BAM !"

Lucas said, as he waved his pretend wand towards his dog Ruffles.

"Oh Ruffles you are supposed to turn into a flying dog."

Lucas SO wanted to be a Wizard.

Suddenly with a flitter and a flap, Magical Master Owl squawked through Lucas's window into the bedroom and explained (in his best owlish) the trouble the wizards were in, and asked a shocked Lucas if he could help.

"Of course!"
said a delighted Lucas.

So Magical Master Owl squawked
three times, flapped his wings
four times, and with a WHIZZ
PUFF, a broomstick, cape and
magic wand suddenly appeared!

Lucas put on the cape, picked up the wand, and jumped on his brand new broomstick.

Quick as a flash they zoomed out of Lucas's window to look for the wicked witch.

11

The wicked witch was flying around, covering everything and everyone with her yucky, smelly green goo.

"Wahahaha!" she cackled, "Soon the whole world will be covered in my smelly goo and there are no wizards here to stop me!"

12

But little did she realize that Lucas was on his way.

He zoomed under bridges...

...and over houses, looking for the goo-spreading witch.

13

Suddenly Ruffles made
a big booming **bark**.
His super-smelling nose had caught
a whiff of the wicked witch, but she
was too far away for **Lucas**
to cast a spell on her.

Lucas clicked
his heels, gripped his
broomstick even tighter,
and zoomed at supersonic speed
towards the wicked witch.

15

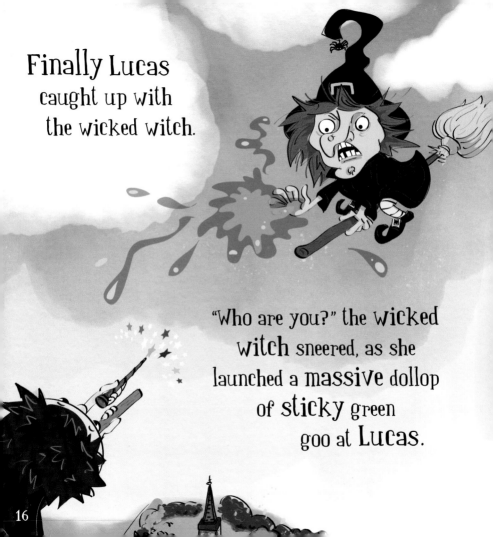

Finally Lucas caught up with the wicked witch.

"Who are you?" the wicked witch sneered, as she launched a massive dollop of sticky green goo at Lucas.

16

With lightning speed
Lucas waved his magic wand.
"BIZZ POP GOO I will stop you!" he shouted.
A huge brightly-colored umbrella appeared,
deflecting all of the smelly goo.

17

The wicked witch squealed with anger, zapping another dollop of smelly green goo towards Lucas.

"WHIZZ SPLAT send me your hat!" Lucas shouted.

The witch's hat flew off her head, catching all of her smelly green goo. Yuck!

The witch couldn't believe what this boy wizard was doing!

18

"ZIP ZAP, you will be trapped in your hat!" Lucas cast another spell.

The witch's goo-filled hat flew back to her, squashing down over her head, squishing her in the smelly green goo.

Hurray the wicked witch was trapped!

19

A triumphant Lucas took the wicked witch back to the wizards' castle.

All the slippery, slimy green goo had now gone thanks to Lucas breaking the bad witch's horrible spell.

20

The wizards were so grateful to
Lucas that they let him keep the cape,
broomstick AND magic wand!

Lucas finally felt like a true wizard!

The End